It's Only Alli Cat

written by
Dandi Daley Knorr

illustrated by
Kathryn Hutton

To my Jenny

Library of Congress Catalog Card Number 89-52032
Copyright ©1990 by Dandi Daley Knorr
Published by The STANDARD PUBLISHING Company, Cincinnati, Ohio
Division of STANDEX INTERNATIONAL Corporation. Printed in U.S.A.

Katy pushed open the door and raced
toward the kitchen. Allyson J. Cat woke
up and stretched until her tummy
rubbed against the carpet.

"Here, Allyson J.!" called Katy.

Katy picked up her pet. Allyson J. Cat had grown since the day Katy had found her in a garbage can behind the house.

"Hello, you two!" greeted Mom. "Did Beth go home, Katy?"

"Yes. But guess what! Our neighborhood is going to have a pet contest! And Beth said the winners get blue ribbons!"

"When is this contest?" asked Mother.

"Sunday afternoon," answered Katy.
"There's a prize for the prettiest pet and
a prize for the most talented pet. Do you
think Allyson J. could win both?"

Mother looked at Ali Cat's shaggy gray fur, skinny tail, and crooked back legs.

"Well," Mother began slowly, "you never know."

The next day was Saturday. Katy
looked out the window and saw Beth
brushing Percy, her Persian cat, in the
yard next door.

"Mom!" yelled Katy. "May I go outside
and see Beth?"

Beth was brushing Percy's long,
white tail as Katy ran up.
"What are you doing?" Katy asked.

"I'm getting Percy ready for the pet show tomorrow. Melissa has a Siamese cat that's really pretty. And Jeff has that fancy Pekingese puppy. But I still think Percy can win."

"Well, I know who I think will win," said Katy.

"Who?" Beth asked.

"I'll be right back and show you," Katy said mysteriously.

Katy returned carrying a small box.
"What's in the box?" asked Beth.
"The winner of Sunday's pet show,"
said Katy with a proud grin.

Katy let Beth look inside the box.

"Oh," laughed Beth. "It's only Ali Cat!"

Katy's grin turned into a frown. She looked at her cat. Allyson's fur stuck out funny. Next to Percy, Allyson J. Cat didn't look like a champion.

"Hey, Katy!" yelled Andrew from across the street. "Watch this!"

Katy looked in time to see Andrew throw a ball into the air. Jake, Andrew's big dog, caught it before it hit the ground.

"Katy, do you think Jake can win the talent prize at the pet show?" asked Andrew.

Katy didn't answer. She was running to find Allyson J. Cat, who had gotten out of her box.

That's it! thought Katy. *I need to teach Allyson J. some tricks. Then I can win the talent prize.*

Katy tried to teach Allyson J. a trick. She told Allyson to lie down, to roll over, to sit up. But Allyson J. Cat just stared.

"It's no use. You can't do anything!" yelled Katy. "You *are* only Ali Cat!"

Sunday morning Katy's family
hurried to get ready for Sunday school.
Katy, who had not even greeted her cat
that morning, rode to church in silence.

The Sunday-school lesson was about a boy named David who was chosen by God to be king. Everyone else thought one of David's brothers should be king because they were big and strong.

But God chose David because he was good *inside*. God didn't need someone who was tall and handsome but someone who was kind and good.

"God doesn't look at the way people are on the outside but the way they are on the *inside*," the teacher said.

Katy took Allyson J. Cat to the pet
show in the afternoon.

"It will be fun!" Mom had said. But
Katy didn't think she would have fun
watching other kids win prizes with
their pets.

Katy sat with Allyson J. on her lap
and watched the show. Charles had a
turtle that could poke its head in and
out of its shell. Erin's dog could shake
hands.

At first, Katy felt sad that she didn't
have a talented pet. But Allyson J. kept
snuggling up to Katy. It was impossible
to stay sad.

Percy did look great. Beth had him in
a new collar and leash. The judge liked
his beautiful white fur.

But just as the judge turned away,
Percy decided he didn't like being on a
leash. He scratched Beth on the arm.
Katy could see Beth starting to cry.

Katy and Ali Cat ran over to see
Beth was okay. Allyson J. rubbed
against Beth and licked her.

"Thanks, Ali Cat," Beth said. Then
she stopped crying.

When the judge announced the
winners, Katy wasn't even
disappointed.

"The award for the 'Most Beautiful
Pet' goes to Beth's cat, Percy." Everyone
clapped.

"And the award for 'Most Talented
Pet' goes to Jeff's talking parrot,
Pirate."

Katy looked at her scraggly cat.

"Allyson J. Cat," she said, "I wouldn't trade you for all the prettiest, most talented pets in the world."

Allyson just purred softly.

"And besides that," said Katy, "you are the prettiest *inside*. And God and I like the inside best."

As Katy got up to leave, she heard the judge announce: "Last, we have a special 'Personality Pet' award for the nicest pet. And the winner is ALLYSON J. CAT."

Katy and Allyson J. got their blue ribbon.

"See," Katy whispered to her cat. "I told you it's what's inside that counts."